Endlessly Ever After

Pick YOUR Path to Countless Fairy Tale Endings!

A story of Little Red Riding Hood, Jack, Hansel, Gretel, Sleeping Beauty, Snow White, a wolf, a witch, a goose, a grandmother, some pigs, and ENDLESS VARIATIONS

LAUREL SNYDER

DAN SANTAT

chronicle books·san francisco

Your mama shakes you out of bed. She says, "My darling dear,
you need to run to Grandma's, quick! She's feeling ill, I fear.

"Now take this cake, to cheer her up, and have a lovely day.
But mind the path! For danger tends to lurk along the way."

So up you jump! You give a nod, and through the room you tear.
But wait, you'll need to grab your coat. It's rather cool out there.

What next, Rosie? *Which coat will you wear?*

To slip on your coziest (faux) fur coat, turn to page 20
To grab your favorite red cape, turn to page 6

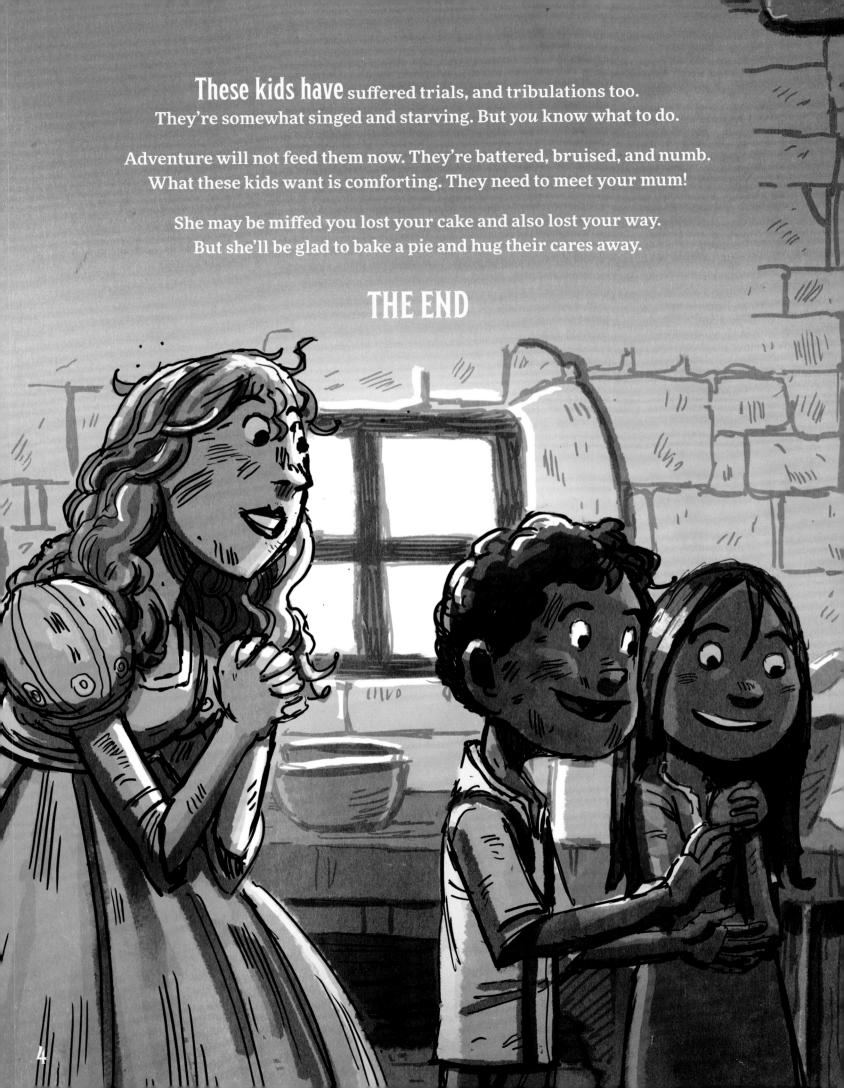

These kids have suffered trials, and tribulations too.
They're somewhat singed and starving. But *you* know what to do.

Adventure will not feed them now. They're battered, bruised, and numb.
What these kids want is comforting. They need to meet your mum!

She may be miffed you lost your cake and also lost your way.
But she'll be glad to bake a pie and hug their cares away.

THE END

4

A wolf is waiting by the path, out in the morning sun.
"I like your fine red cape," he says. "You heading someplace fun?"

"I'm off to see my grandma," you tell your toothy friend.
"Her house is purple, with a gate, down at the very end.

"I haven't time to chat just now. I've got a ways to walk.
But have a lovely afternoon. Another time, we'll talk!"

The wolf just nods his furry head and quickly slips away.
He flicks his tail and disappears into the sunny day.

And standing on the path alone, you fear you've been unwise.
You can't forget his claws or jaws, his shifty yellow eyes.

You wish you hadn't met that wolf. You wish he didn't know
exactly how you plan to walk and where you mean to go.

Now what, Rosie? *Are you going to let that wolf scare you away from your adventure?*

YES, silly. Wolves are no joke! To go back inside and start fresh tomorrow, turn to page 2

To take a deep breath and journey on, turn to page 50

The somber drumbeat leads you to a coffin in a glen.
Inside you find a maiden fair. Around it, seven men.

The drummer stops and waves hello, then reaches for your cake.
"So kind of you to come," he says. "We'll serve this at the wake."

You're not quite certain what to do—you don't mean to be *rude*,
but you don't know this pretty girl. And that's your grandma's food!

Now what, Rosie? *Are you going to let those dwarfs take Grandma's goodies?*

It's only cake, and they're really sad! To let them have the treat, turn to page 66
No way! You've already wasted too much time. To grab your cake and head to
Grandma's, turn to page 54

These roses are so lovely, but every single stem
is covered in sharp prickle-pins. It hurts to gather them!

When suddenly, the vines all part and make a door for you!
Of course you want to step inside, but is that smart to do?

How do you dare to enter this castle of a home?
And yet, how can you bear to leave where magic seems to roam?

What next, Rosie? *Are you really so afraid of magic?*

To pass the thorns and enter the castle, turn to page 42
To back away, turn to page 64

You knock and wait and knock, and then you knock a little more.
At last a window opens up! "Is someone at my door?"

"It's me," you call. "It's Rosie! I came to say hello."
At that, the pig begins to shriek: "The wolf's returned. OH, NO!"

"You've got it wrong," you try to say. "I'm not a wolf, not me.
I'm just a girl inside a coat. I'll take it off. You'll see!"

But *then*, of course, your zipper's stuck. (Sometimes life isn't fair.)
And as you struggle with the zip, large objects fill the air.

As dishes rain, and furniture, the piggy gives a cry.
"I'll take revenge for Oink and Boink. *You*, vile wolf, must die!"

And though you turn to run away, there isn't time for that.
You're finished off in seconds, and you never hear the SPLAT.

THE END

You bravely dash into the woods! You hunt the hunter down
and find him standing by a heap of wolf upon the ground.

"Hello there, girl!" the hunter calls. "Aren't you a lucky pup.
If you'd come any sooner, he might have chewed you up!"

You really don't know what to say. He's holding poor Jack's goose.
It's awful dead, without a head, and feathers coming loose.

And yet, you're glad the wolf is gone. You really can't pretend.
You're grateful to the hunter, although he robbed your friend.

"Umm, thanks, I guess," you stammer, then turn and walk away.
You're feeling so bewildered by this crazy mixed-up day.

You aren't sure of anything. What's good? What's bad? And why?
You guess it's time to head on home. You hope Mum's baking pie. . . .

THE END

What sort of girl would want to chase a somber beating drum?
It makes you think of marching feet. It makes the woods feel glum.

You'd rather gather bluebells, collect some daisies too.
But don't take long. You need to go. Your gran's expecting you.

However, as you turn to leave, you notice, through the trees,
a vine of bright red roses (and big fat bumblebees).

You've never seen such blossoms. Your gran loves roses so.
But you're already running late. Oh my, which way to go?

Now what, Rosie? *Is it worth it? Do you really need even more flowers?*

To stop and gather the roses, turn to page 10
To get back on the path and hurry along to Gran's as quickly as possible, turn to page 34

You take one tiny nibble. You lick . . . and chew . . . and bite.
It's extra yummy, gooey-gummy. Crisp and rich and light.

Until you hear a cackle! A shout of witchy glee!
You find you're caught in licorice. You try to wriggle free.

But it's no use. You're stuck for good. No matter how you rage,
you're trapped forever in a magic candy-coated cage.

THE END

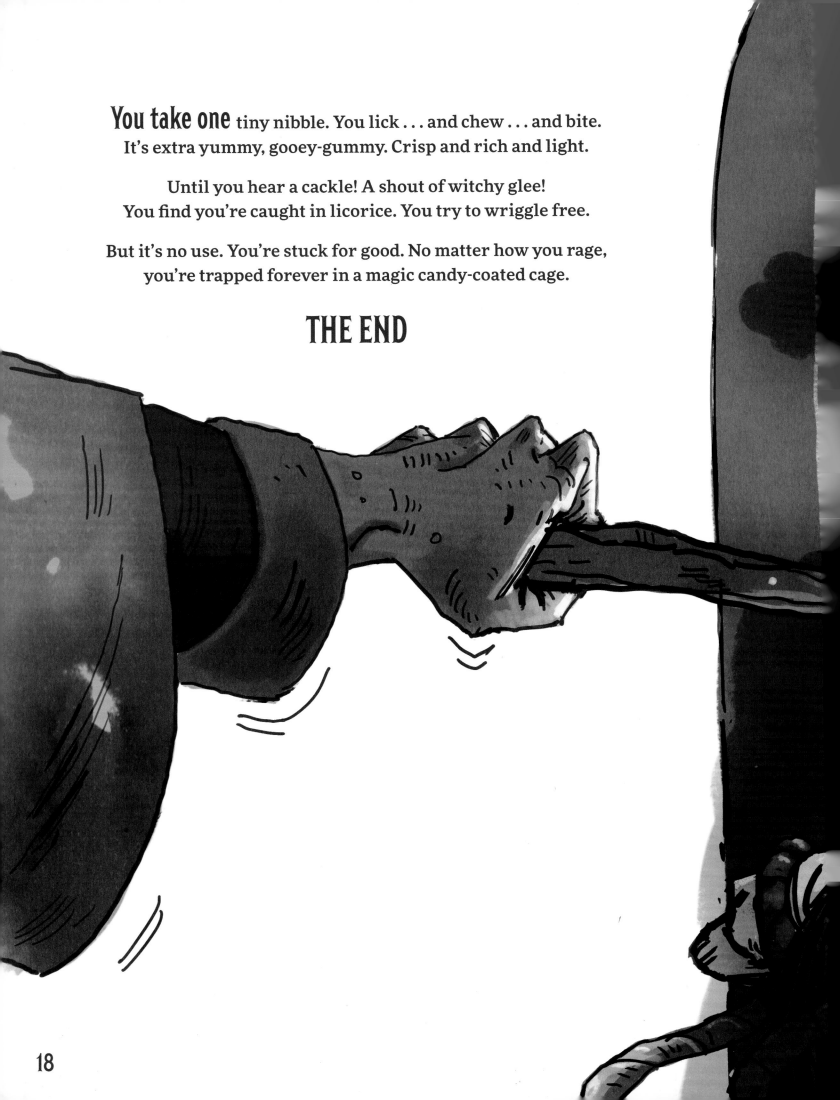

Inside your coat, as warm as toast, you skip through every glade.
You'll soon be at your grandma's house and sipping lemonade.

But when you get to "down the path," you find you're somewhere new.
A house you've never seen before. It's brick, the door bright blue.

You know your gran is waiting. She's sick and stuck abed.
But would it hurt to quickly knock on this fine door instead?

Now what, Rosie? *Are you going to knock on this completely unfamiliar door?*

You've wasted plenty of time already, and you know it.

To hurry on to Grandma's house, turn to page 44
To stop for just a minute and meet your neighbors, turn to page 12

"My darling dear," growls Granny. "Come closer, near to me!
And don't be scared by my big eyes. I need them both to see."

"Your hands are funny too," you say. "The cabin light's so dim.
And yet I fear you look all wrong. You've whiskers on your chin."

"Now that's not nice," snaps Granny. "It isn't kind to say
such things about a lady. Someday you'll look this way."

"But oh, your ears are pointy. And also very big!"
Your granny grins. "They help me hear. Now don't you fret a fig."

The floor creaks as you take two steps. The candle flares and flits.
And suddenly you realize: You're scared out of your wits.

What next, Rosie? *What are you going to do this time?*

To walk forward and kiss your granny like a good girl, turn to page 62
To follow your instincts, turn, and dash for the door, turn to page 38

You step a little closer. You ask, "Are you okay?
You look upset and sopping wet. I'm Rosie, by the way."

"Hello," he says. "My name is Jack. I'm not okay at all.
Some awful hunter stole my pants, and boots, and that's not all—
while I was bathing in the creek, he also took my goose!
I only hope she manages to somehow wriggle loose.

"He ran in that direction. I don't know what to do.
When Mum finds out I lost our bird, she'll put me in the stew.

"I don't suppose you'll help me? Go see if you can find that hunter, and retrieve my clothes? I'm in an awful bind."

What next, Rosie? *Are you really going to head off on a wild goose chase?*

To apologize kindly but head along home, turn to page 64
To do the kid a favor, turn to page 60

25

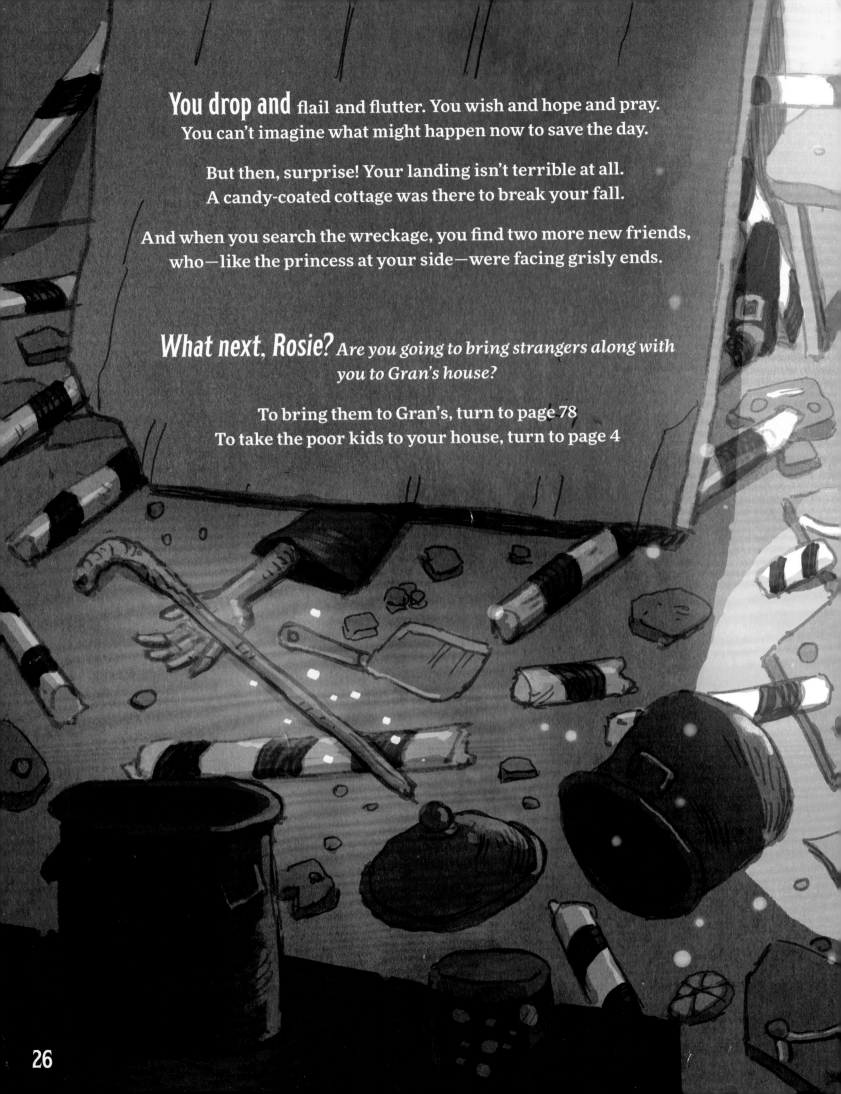

You drop and flail and flutter. You wish and hope and pray.
You can't imagine what might happen now to save the day.

But then, surprise! Your landing isn't terrible at all.
A candy-coated cottage was there to break your fall.

And when you search the wreckage, you find two more new friends,
who—like the princess at your side—were facing grisly ends.

What next, Rosie? *Are you going to bring strangers along with
you to Gran's house?*

To bring them to Gran's, turn to page 78
To take the poor kids to your house, turn to page 4

Of course you say, "No thanks," and run, as fast as you can flee.
You get so hot you have to hang your coat up on a tree.

But since you've stopped, you think you'll sit and take a tiny rest.
And when you do, somehow the sun slips quickly to the west.

At last you wake. It's gotten late. You have to go now, quick!
You scurry over to the path, but which way should you pick?

Now what, Rosie? *You really shouldn't have taken that nap.*
Now you've lost your way!

To try THIS WAY, turn to page 76
To head along THAT WAY, turn to page 34

You've got no choice. You sit and wait. It's dark, and what a bore!
You're not quite sure if this is death. You've never died before!

It *smells* like death, like moldy socks. It feels all warm and wet.
If you're heading for heaven, you haven't left just yet.

But then, beyond the darkness, a voice cries, "Wolf, BEGONE!"
You hear some smacks, some cracks, some whacks! And all the lights come on!

What next, Rosie? *What a day! Are you ready to go home yet?*

To learn a nice moral, turn to page 69
To walk home slowly and think about things, turn to page 64

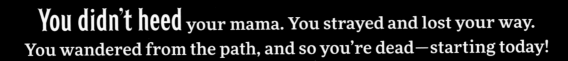

You didn't heed your mama. You strayed and lost your way.
You wandered from the path, and so you're dead—starting today!

In front of you, a tunnel—a long, dark, winding hall.
You see a light there at the end. You wonder at it all.

It's time to head along that path, to march on toward the light.
You know you shouldn't stray again. And yet, you fear you *might*. . . .

THE END

You dash along the path and soon arrive at Granny's gate.
"Come in!" she calls. And yet you don't. You halt. You hesitate. . . .

Because her voice sounds different. All breathy, hoarse, and low.
Down deep inside, you long to hide. Or maybe turn and go.

What next, Rosie? *You finally got to Grandma's, and now you want to leave?*

To go in and visit your grandmother like a good girl, turn to page 22
To follow your instincts and run like heck, turn to page 76

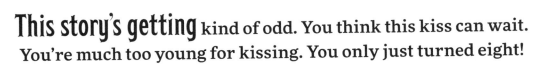

This story's getting kind of odd. You think this kiss can wait.
You're much too young for kissing. You only just turned eight!

And once beyond the castle walls, you find you've left your cake.
So you turn 'round and trot on home. But with each step you take . . .

you wonder at that girl asleep, inside her walls of stone.
And you will wonder all your days at what you *might* have done.

THE END

You turn to run. You try to flee. You leap to reach the door. But as you do the wolf leaps too. With such an awful roar!

You give a kick. You raise a fist! You shout and shake and fight.
You reach and grab a skillet, and hurl with all your might. . . .

And when it thunks that nasty wolf, he howls and shouts out, "No!"
He slinks away, brought low and meek, by your one angry blow.

You've rescued YOU, all on your own. You're both savee and saver.
That wolf's a wimp, and now you know: Big teeth don't make you braver!

THE END

The moment that you charge the queen, she gives a wicked smile
and hurls her potion at your feet. Strange smoke pours from the vial!

You feel a cloud surround you, an awful evil breeze.
A force descends upon your limbs, and all your muscles freeze.

The room now smells like roses, but something darker too.
Like stormy nights and lost goodbyes . . . as sleep envelopes you.

You may have choices someday and further paths to tread,
but they're not in *this* story. You sleep as if you're dead.

THE END (for now)

You wander up a winding stair; you scamper past a throne,
until you find a tiny room, where sleeping like a stone,

a gentle maiden waits for you. Her eyes are sweetly shut.
Her lips are waiting for a kiss. And so you bend and . . . WHAT?

Now what, Rosie? *Are you really going to kiss some strange sleeping woman
in a frozen castle covered with roses? Seriously?*

Yes, life is an adventure! Turn to page 48
No, ew! Of course not. Kissing's for teenagers. Turn to page 36

Your grandma's waiting for her cake. You will not let her down.
But as you near her cottage, a shadow hits the ground.

A wolf has found you, gives a grin. "My furry friend, let's flee!
I bet you're headed where I am, the deep-woods jamboree?

"We're sure to find delicious treats and wolfish games galore.
Why don't you wander off the path? Such fun we have in store!"

What next, Rosie? *That sounds like fun! Are you going to go with him?*

To head along with your new furry friend, turn to page 47
To avoid the wolfish invitation and head on to Grandma's, turn to page 28

OHMYGOSH, YOU DID IT! You kissed the princess fair,
who softly stirs and yawns at you through endless yards of hair.

But then her big eyes widen. She cries, "Oh, no! The queen!"
And sure enough, a woman waits behind you. She looks *mean*!

"You know you should be napping!" the evil queen exclaims.
She conjures up a potion, unstoppers it, and aims—

What next, Rosie? *Are you really going to take on that evil queen?*

To run at that queen and try to grab her potion, turn to page 40
To duck and dodge, while you think up a plan, turn to page 71

49

You will not let that mean old wolf destroy your lovely day.
That furry bully has no right to bother you this way.

But you've a care for safety, and so you shed your hood.
The sun is bright, and you'll be fine. It's warm now in the wood.

The smell of flowers fills the air, so fragrant and so sweet.
But then you notice there's a sound, a somber steady beat.

You know your grandma's waiting. But *she'll* be home all day.
You've got some time to wander. The question is . . . which way?

What next, Rosie?
What should you do with your extra minutes?

To gather some fragrant flowers for Grandma, turn to page 16
To follow the sound of the beating drum, turn to page 8

You hate his ugly, greedy grin. It's just too much to bear.
You run to punch him in the gut, and grab him by the hair.

He gives a mighty howl! But then . . . he gets his claws on you—
and then his jaws!—he chews you up as wolves are known to do.

THE END

You shake your head. "I have to leave, or Mama will be miffed.
I'm sorry that your friend is dead. I hope your spirits lift."

But once you're back upon the path, you hear an angry shout.
Somewhere a boy is bellowing. You wonder what about.

You've wasted too much time today. You really need to fly.
But in your gut, you wonder what, and who, and how, and why?

What next, Rosie? *First a drumbeat and now a shout?*
Are you really going to waste more time?

To ignore the noise and run straight to Gran's, turn to page 34
Who are you kidding? You have to know what all the yelling is about!
Turn to page 56

54

You head off through the trees again. You track the shouts of rage
and find them coming from a kid, a boy about your age.

He kicks and shouts and punches. He bellows and he rants.
He's also dripping wet and wears a frown and underpants.

You blush until your face is red. You want to run away,
but then, you're also curious. How did he get this way?

Now what, Rosie? *Are you really going to hang around
with this wet, pantsless boy?*

To head home now and avoid this ridiculous mess altogether, turn to page 64
To ask what's wrong and help this poor kid, turn to page 24

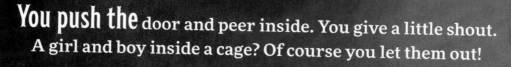

You push the door and peer inside. You give a little shout.
A girl and boy inside a cage? Of course you let them out!

"An evil witch, she trapped us! She means to make *kid* stew!
We have to run. *You* have to come, or else she'll nosh you too!"

You sprint home quick to Mama. You climb inside your bed.
The world is full of awful things. You'll read a book instead.

THE END

You quickly take your jerkin off and hand it straight to Jack.
The poor boy's nearly naked. "No need to give it back."

And after that you walk a ways; you climb a little hill.
From there, you can see everything. A bridge. A fort. A mill.

You spy your grandma's cottage. A stream, a pretty lake,
and, everywhere, the winding path. So many turns to take.

It's nice to rest a minute, to stop and think a bit.
To see the world around you, and slowly ponder it.

Until you spot a fluttering—a pale thing in the wood!
Could that be Jack's beloved goose? Or is it gone for good?

And somewhere else below you, a man's voice fills the air.
"A-hunting we will go!" he sings. "Be tasty—and BEWARE!"

Now what, Rosie? *You aren't sure what to do! Which direction should you go?*

To follow the ominous hunting song, turn to page 14
To chase the vague white flutter that might be a goose, turn to page 72

60

You step up to your granny's bed. "Oh, gosh," you say. "Your . . . tooth?"
(When "snarly-snaggle-dagger" is closer to the truth.)

"This little thing?" growls Granny. "Don't fret. I've got a hunch
that *this* will come in handy . . . WHEN I EAT YOU FOR LUNCH!!!"

At that she leaps and howls and tears the covers from her bed.
She gives one chomp. The world goes dark. You think you must be dead.

What next, Rosie? *Not much you can do this time, huh?*

To twiddle your thumbs and wait to see what happens next, turn to page 30
To chew your fingernails and wait to see what happens next, turn to page 32

63

This day has been too much for you, and so you turn to go.
You stroll along that same old path. You take it extra slow.

As evening falls, you notice folks all heading different ways.
You watch them walk and wonder . . . what happened in *their* days?

THE END

You know it's nice to share your treats, and these guys seem so glum.
So you step forward right away. You mean to give them some.

But as you offer up the cake, you trip against the casket
and stub your toe and stumble—and drop your picnic basket.

Just then an odd thing happens. When jostled by the cake,
the girl for whom you're mourning appears to give a shake.

She coughs and opens both her eyes. She blinks there in her bed.
"I'm awful glad to see you here. I thought that I was dead."

So then the wake becomes a feast. The birds and deer demand
to sing and prance and celebrate. Your gran will understand. . . .

THE END

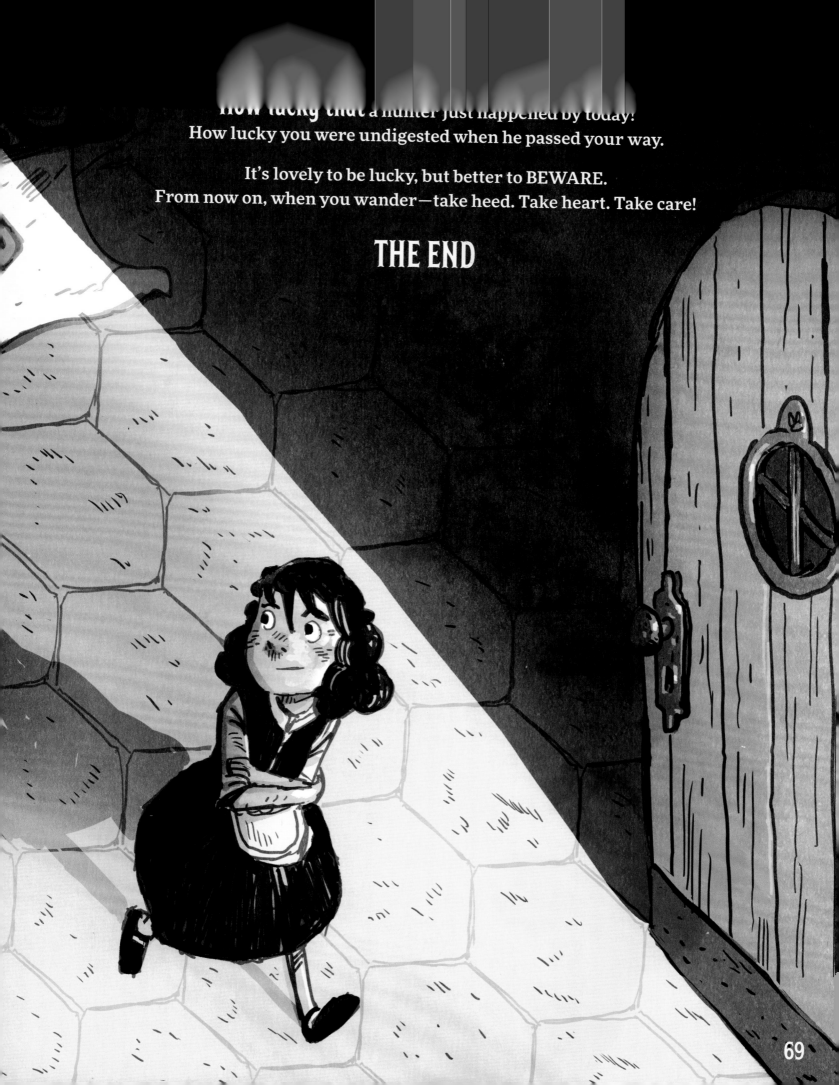

How lucky that a hunter just happened by today!
How lucky you were undigested when he passed your way.

It's lovely to be lucky, but better to BEWARE.
From now on, when you wander—take heed. Take heart. Take care!

THE END

You duck and dodge, and just in time!
The queen runs straight at you.
But you think fast and trip her up—she stumbles on your shoe.

The potion tumbles from her hand, and cinders fill the room.
It smells like last year's roses. Like rain and ash and doom.

So you head for the window, and leap into the air.
You'd like to pick another path, but fate awaits down there.

Now what, Rosie? *You're jumping out a window.*
Do you really want to see what happens next?

To leap with your eyes open, turn to page 26
To leap with your eyes closed, turn to page 74

With princess fingers clutched in yours, you squeeze your eyes so tight.
And all the choices you have left? They disappear from sight.

You do not get to pick your path when falling through the air.
When gravity's in charge, the only option is DOWN THERE.

You don't have time to chat and learn about your new best friend.
In reaching out for her today, you've also reached . . .

THE END

You run until you find a house you've never seen before.
With choco-coated gummy bits all stuck above the door.

The porch is made of toffee. There are no bricks. Instead,
the walls are glazed with caramel and built of gingerbread.

You knock at once. You whistle. You wait. And wonder. And . . .
at last you try the knob and find it breaks off in your hand.

You know someone must live here. It isn't yours to taste.
But oh, it smells delicious. It shouldn't go to waste.

Where did this cottage come from? How did you get waylaid?
You swear you never left the path. You're not sure how you strayed!

What next, Rosie?

Surely you can take one little bite. Right?

To take a wee little bite of the knob, turn to page 18
To step inside and have a look around, turn to page 59

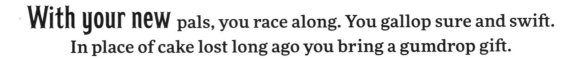

With your new pals, you race along. You gallop sure and swift.
In place of cake lost long ago you bring a gumdrop gift.

You pass a piggy on a hunt for mushrooms in the wood.
You pass a goose boy looking sad. "My goose is gone for good!"

And when you get to Granny's house, you see before the door
a furry and familiar form. A face you've seen before.

He growls at you, "Where have you been? I waited half the day.
You should have been here hours ago. I almost went away!"

"What did you do with Granny?" you ask the wicked beast.
He licks his chops. He grins and says, "She made a lovely feast."

So now you look to your new pals. The princess shrugs at you.
And Hansel's lost, and Gretel seems to be without a clue.

It's time somebody trounced this wolf. It's time for him to go.
But how, and what's a girl to do? It's awful hard to know. . . .

Now what, Rosie?

To charge the wolf, turn to page 52
To whack him with your new walking stick, turn to page 80

The second that you raise your stick, the big bad wolf begins
to leap, and on his face you see the greediest of grins.

You fear you may have reached THE END. You cringe and squint your eyes.
But in that final moment, you bonk him, and—SURPRISE!

The wolf's no danger to you now. In fact, he looks quite sweet,
made all of fudge and candy floss—a giant doggy treat!

And even better, here comes Gran—she's not the least bit dead!
She only had a goose to pluck, out back, behind the shed.

She asks you and your friends to stay and have a little lunch.
But you decline and say goodbye. You've got a mighty hunch . . .

(This choice is easy. Just turn the page. . . .)

. . . **that somewhere** waiting down the path there's even more to see.
You've got to know how fierce or fun or far that *more* might be.

And as you wander off beneath a slowly sinking sun,
you sense adventure down the path. Your journey's just begun.

Some people sleep and drift and dream their stories all away.
Some people like to mind the path
or stay at home to play.
But whether you adventure far
or sit alone
or snooze,

the thing you must remember is

that every day . . .